This book belongs to

Melissa Diaz

Por Alessandra

DISNEY · PIXAR
TOY STORY 2

A READ-ALOUD STORYBOOK

Adapted by Kathleen Zoehfeld

MOUSE WORKS

Visit www.ToyStory2.com
A part of the GO Network.

Printed in the United States of America.

ISBN 0-7364-0151-2

WOODY GETS STOLEN

When his arm tore, Woody couldn't go to Cowboy Camp with Andy.

"Woody's been shelved!" cried Mr. Potato Head.

3

The next morning, Sarge yelled, "Red alert!" Andy's mom was having a yard sale.

When a toy penguin was taken to the sale Woody rode Andy's puppy to the rescue!

But as the puppy ran back to the house, Woody fell to the ground!

Helplessly, Buzz Lightyear watched a toy collector steal Woody and drive away.

At the collector's apartment, Woody met Bullseye the horse and Jessie the cowgirl.

"And say hello to the Prospector," said Jessie. "He's mint in the box. Never been opened."

"It's good to see you, Woody," said the Prospector.

"How do you know my name?" asked Woody. Then he saw his own face on the cover of a magazine.

When Jessie put a tape in the VCR, an announcer hollered, "Welcome to *Woody's Roundup*!" Woody had been a TV star!

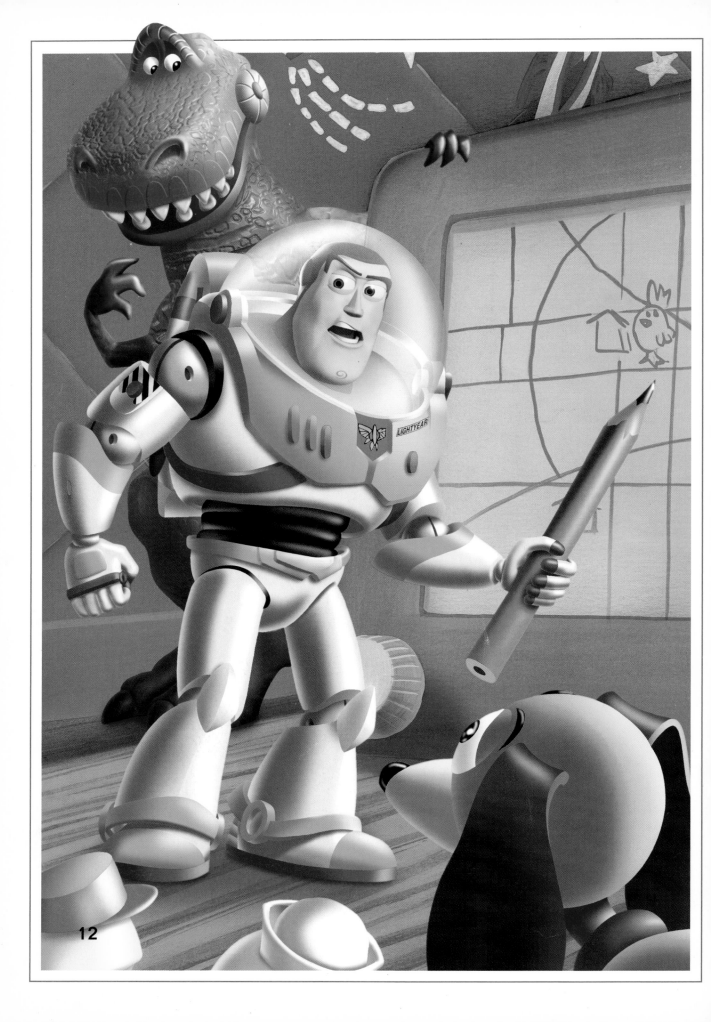

BUZZ TO THE RESCUE

Back home, Buzz, Slinky, Mr. Potato Head, Hamm, and Rex set out to rescue Woody. They had recognized the man who stole Woody from a TV commercial.

"To Al's Toy Barn and beyond!" declared Buzz.

Woody was having fun playing with his new friends, but they all froze when Al walked into the room.

Al was gloating about how much money he could sell Woody for, when . . . *RIP!* Woody's arm tore off!

Woody was still determined to get home. When Al fell asleep, he tried to escape.

BLARE! The television blasted on. Woody froze as Al woke up. Then Woody noticed the TV remote control. Had one of his new friends turned on the TV?

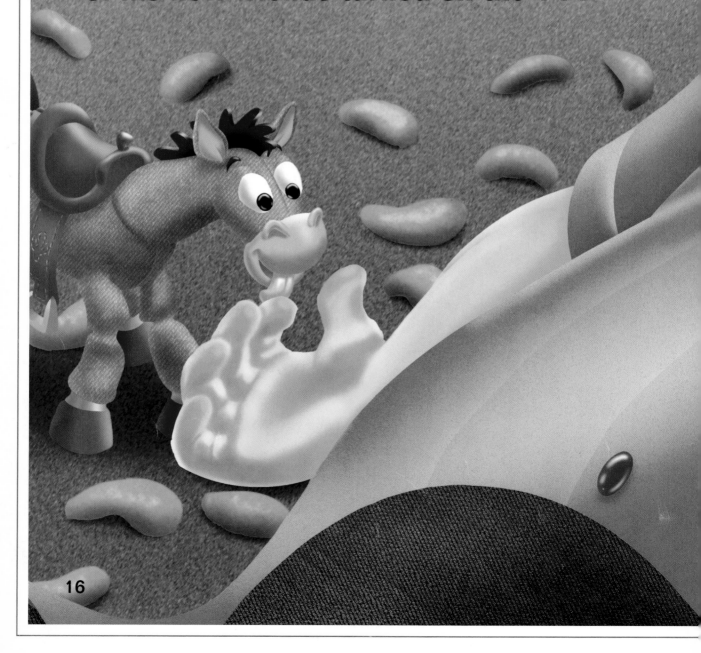

17

By that time, Buzz and the others had reached a busy, four-lane highway. "We have to find a way to cross," said Buzz.

Five orange traffic cones trotted across, sending the traffic every which way.

"Ah, that went well," said Mr. Potato Head.

"Good job, troops," said Buzz. "We're that much closer to Woody."

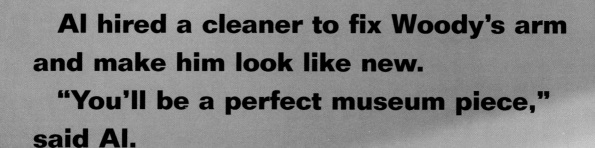

Al hired a cleaner to fix Woody's arm and make him look like new.

"You'll be a perfect museum piece," said Al.

Finally Buzz and the other brave toys reached their destination—Al's Toy Barn. The toys split up to look for Woody.

Down one aisle, Buzz discovered—a new Buzz!

"You're breaking ranks, Ranger," declared the new Buzz. When they tussled, the new Buzz twist-tied Andy's Buzz in a box and crammed him on the shelf.

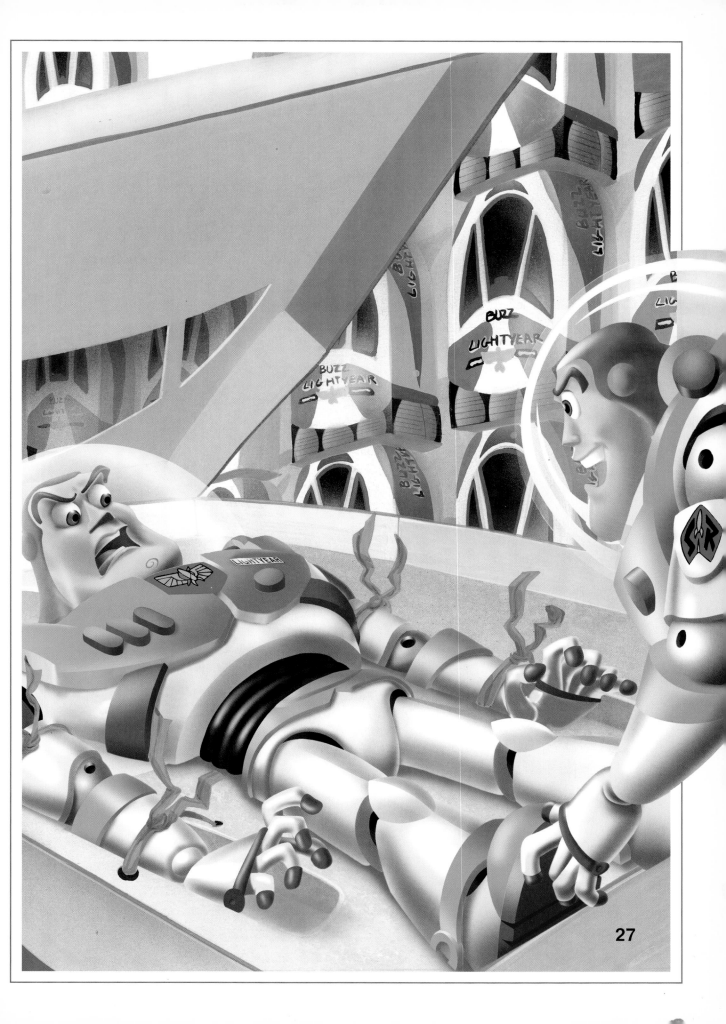

Soon the other toys arrived in a sports car. "I found a manual that shows how to defeat Zurg!" said Rex, talking about the video game he could never win.

"Let's go!" shouted the new Buzz—he was ready to battle Zurg for the safety of the universe!

30

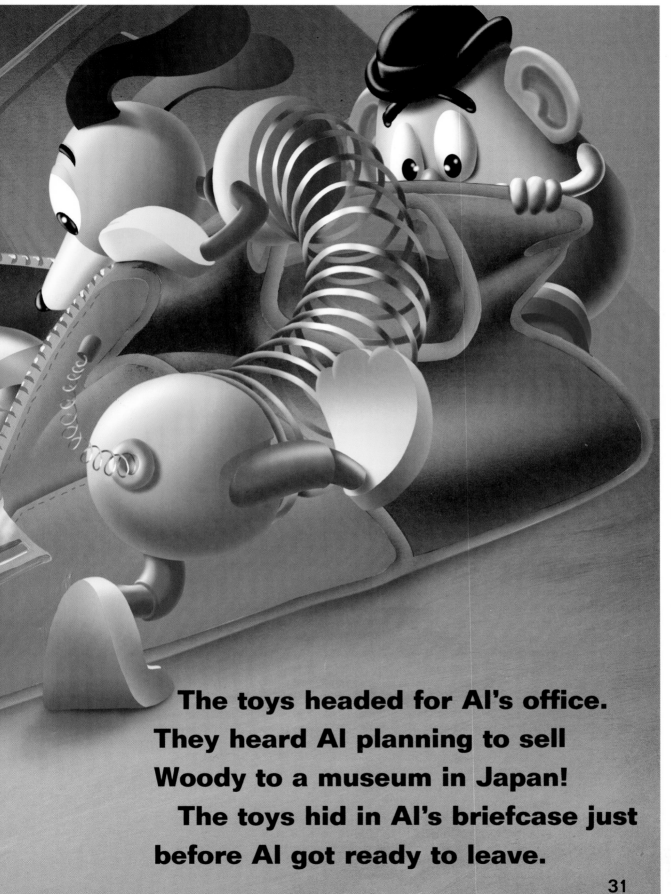

The toys headed for Al's office.
They heard Al planning to sell
Woody to a museum in Japan!
The toys hid in Al's briefcase just
before Al got ready to leave.

31

Andy's Buzz escaped from the box and hurried after Al. Buzz didn't notice that a Zurg toy had burst out of its box and was following him!

The toys followed Al into his apartment building.

"We can climb through here," said the new Buzz, pointing to an air vent. Finally, the toys broke through the vent leading into Al's apartment!

"We're here to spring you, Woody!"
cried Slinky.

Then Andy's Buzz arrived. To prove
that he was the real Buzz, he lifted his
boot. In thick black marker on the
bottom was the name ANDY!

"Let's go, Woody," said Buzz.

To his surprise, Woody said, "I'm a rare collectible. I belong in a museum."

"You . . . are . . . a . . . toy!" Buzz shouted, but Woody refused to leave.

As the toys left, Woody thought about his old life. "I'm supposed to be played with," he decided. "I have to get home!" But the Prospector stood in his way.

From the vent, Buzz watched as Al returned and packed Woody in his bag.

41

"We gotta get Woody! He changed his mind!" cried Buzz. But the toys ran right into . . . Zurg!

A battle broke out between the Buzzes and Zurg.

As Rex turned away, his tail knocked Zurg into the elevator shaft. "I finally defeated Zurg!" cheered Rex.

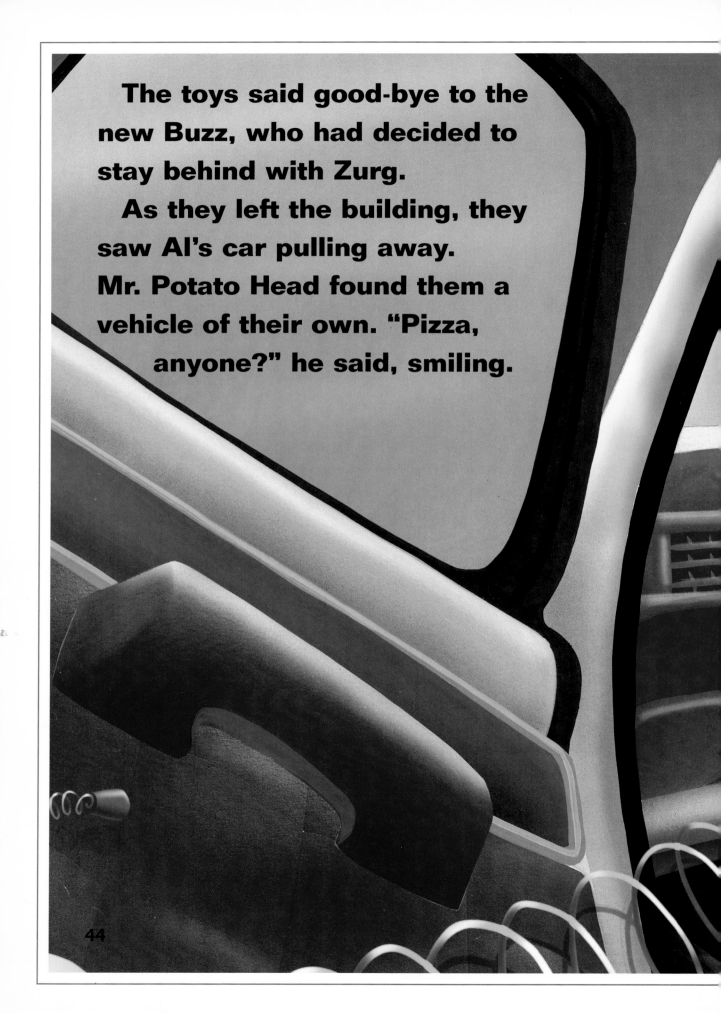

The toys said good-bye to the new Buzz, who had decided to stay behind with Zurg.

As they left the building, they saw Al's car pulling away. Mr. Potato Head found them a vehicle of their own. "Pizza, anyone?" he said, smiling.

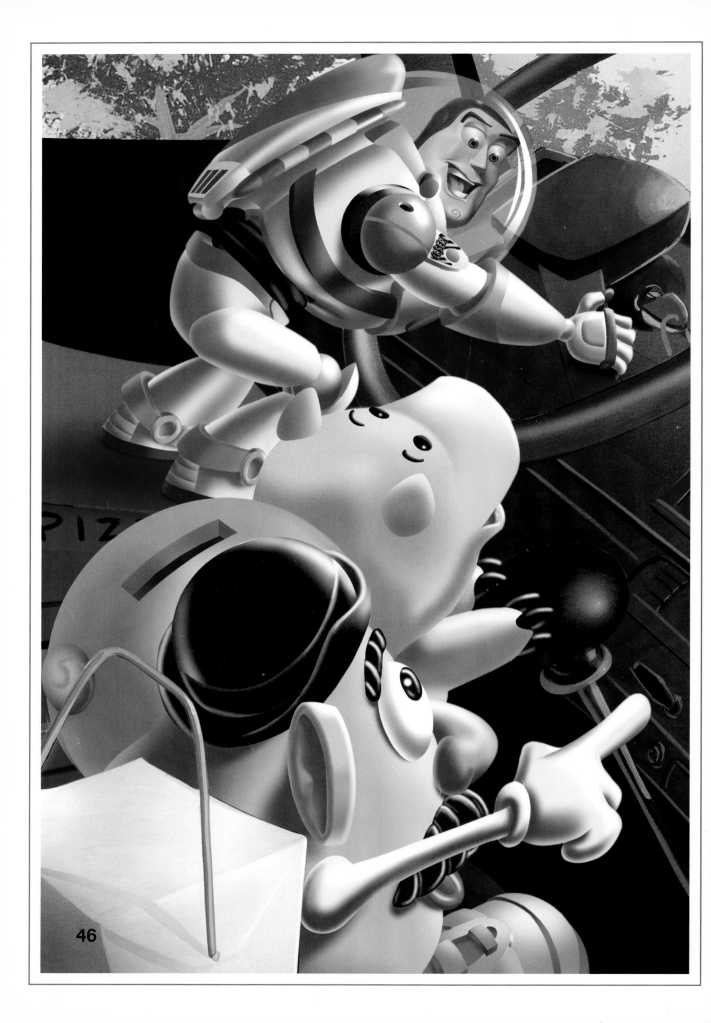

THE AIRPORT CHASE

Barreling down the highway in a Pizza Planet truck, the toys followed Al all the way to the airport.

As Al headed into the terminal, Buzz spotted a pet carrier. "There's the perfect camouflage!" he said.

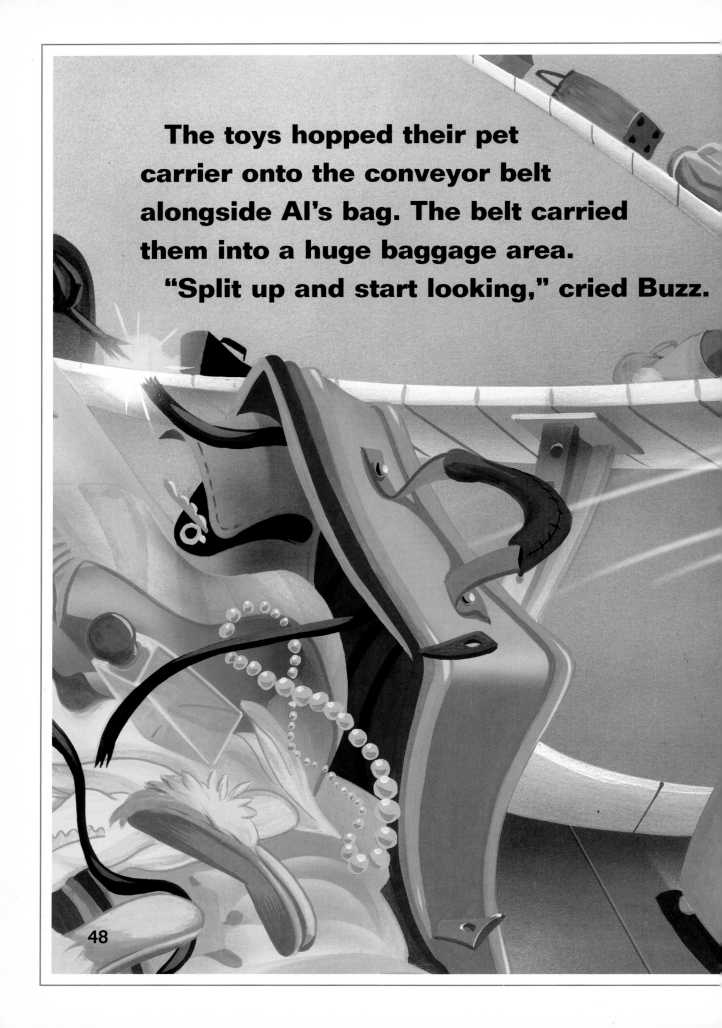

The toys hopped their pet carrier onto the conveyor belt alongside Al's bag. The belt carried them into a huge baggage area.

"Split up and start looking," cried Buzz.

Opening one bag, Buzz found . . . an angry Prospector! Woody escaped from his case and helped Buzz stuff the Prospector into a passing backpack.

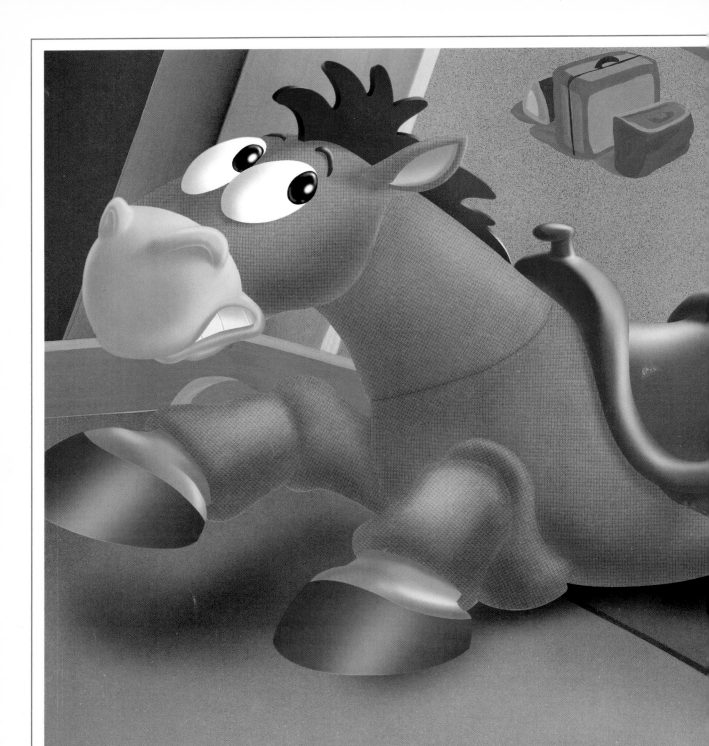

Next, Bullseye struggled free from the case, but Jessie was still trapped inside. Woody and Buzz jumped onto Bullseye's back.

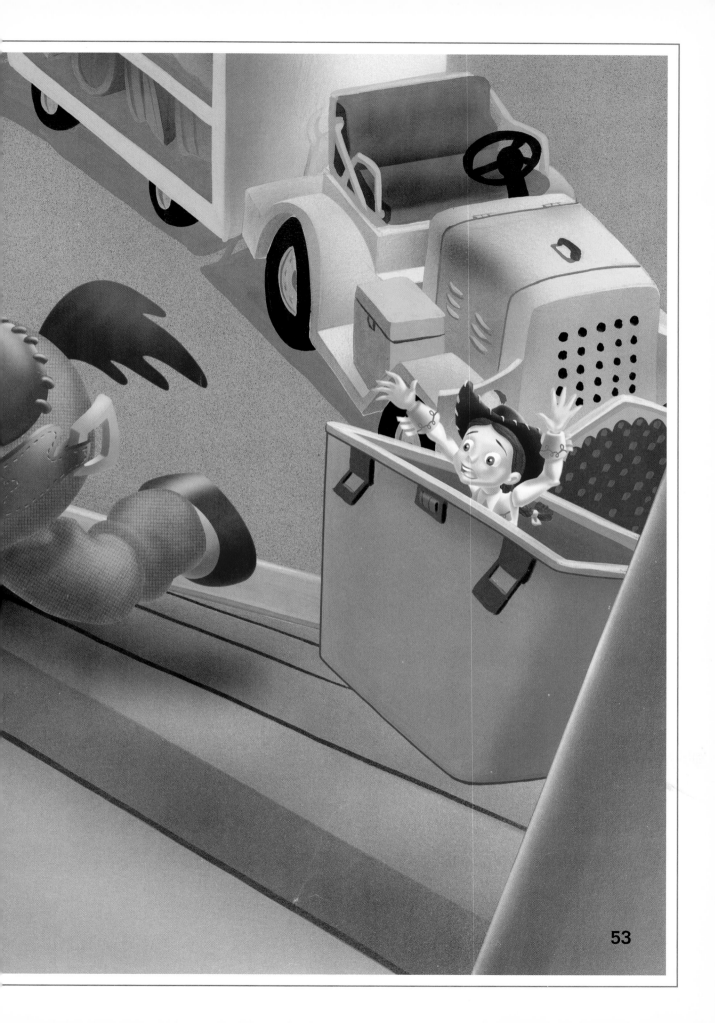

"Yee-ha! Giddy-up!" Woody shouted.
Then he jumped from Bullseye's back
to the baggage train that was carrying
Jessie away.

But Woody wasn't able to rescue Jessie. They were both loaded onto the plane—and the plane was about to take off!

From inside the plane, Woody and Jessie tried to escape through the landing gear.

"You can't have a rescue without Buzz Lightyear," cried Buzz. He rode Bullseye under the plane—Woody and Jessie jumped to safety!

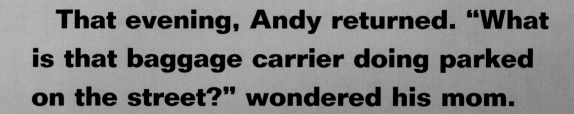

That evening, Andy returned. "What is that baggage carrier doing parked on the street?" wondered his mom.

Andy burst into his room. The first thing he did was look for Woody.

"Howdy, pardner!" he said. Then he spotted Bullseye and Jessie. "New toys! Thanks, Mom!" he cried.

And from that time on, Woody and his friends were happy not to be stuck on a museum shelf. They were real toys—played with and loved.